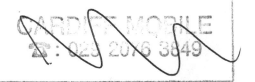

Nipper McFee

In Trouble with Mrs McFee

For Rosa
R.I.

For Connor
M.W.

Reading Consultant: Prue Goodwin, Lecturer in literacy and children's books

ORCHARD BOOKS
338 Euston Road, London NW1 3BH
Orchard Books Australia
Hachette Children's Books
Level 17/207 Kent Street, Sydney NSW 2000

First published in 2011 by Orchard Books

Text © Rose Impey 2011
Illustrations © Melanie Williamson 2011

ISBN 978 1 40830 220 0 (hardback)
ISBN 978 1 40830 228 6 (paperback)

1 3 5 7 9 10 8 6 4 2 (hardback)
1 3 5 7 9 10 8 6 4 2 (paperback)

Printed in China

Orchard Books is a division of Hachette Children's Books,
an Hachette UK company.

www.hachette.co.uk

Nipper McFee

In Trouble with **Mrs McFee**

Written by ROSE IMPEY

Illustrated by MELANIE WILLIAMSON

ORCHARD BOOKS

Nipper McFee was often in trouble,
but this time it was *serious*!

Nipper and his friends, Will and
Lil, were having fun. They were
throwing water bombs at their old
enemies, the basement rats, when…

Great Aunt Twitter stepped out
of the Fabulous Fur Parlour and
got caught in the crossfire.

"Now we're in trouble," said Lil.

When PC Poodle brought Nipper
home, Mrs McFee was furious.
She said it was the *final straw!*

"You're grounded," she told Nipper.

"For how long?" he asked, nervously.

"*For ever,*" yelled his mother.

Nipper had never seen her this
mad before.

By four o'clock the next day Nipper
thought he would die of boredom!
He decided to run away – to sea.

10

His grandpa, Captain Cornish
McCray, had fought with pirates.
That was the life for Nipper.

Nipper hoped his friends would
run away with him.
But Will said, "Sorry, it's Friday."
"Kippers and chips for supper," said Lil.
It was their favourite.

Will and Lil wished Nipper luck
and waved him goodbye.
Nipper set off with his little
rucksack, hoping to leave trouble
far behind him.

But, hidden round the corner,
trouble watched Nipper leave
and decided to follow.

"If Nipper goes," the rats asked
themselves, "who else will we tease
and torment?"
They planned to bring Nipper back,
whether he liked it or not.

It was getting dark by the time
Nipper reached the docks.
A large ship was waiting, almost
ready to set sail.

Nipper checked that no one
was looking before he sneaked
on board.

Then he went below,
looking for a place
to stow away.

But soon *trouble* followed hot
on his heels.

Down in the hold Nipper found a
good place to hide. There was even
a hammock.
But it was very dark and he started
to feel a bit scared.

18

BOOTY

STASH

Nipper tried to be brave.
He tried to imagine all the
adventures he would have fighting
bloodthirsty pirates – just like
his grandpa!

Meanwhile, above his head, the rats
were racing round the ship,
searching for Nipper.
As usual, they made trouble
wherever they went.

They caused damage on the
decks, a stampede on the stairs
and chaos in the kitchen.
Fire alarms went off on every floor.

But Nipper didn't hear anything.
He was lying in his hammock
feeling a little homesick.

Good food smells were coming from the kitchen. They reminded Nipper of his mother's roly-poly pudding. Nipper was hungry, but at least his troubles were far behind him.

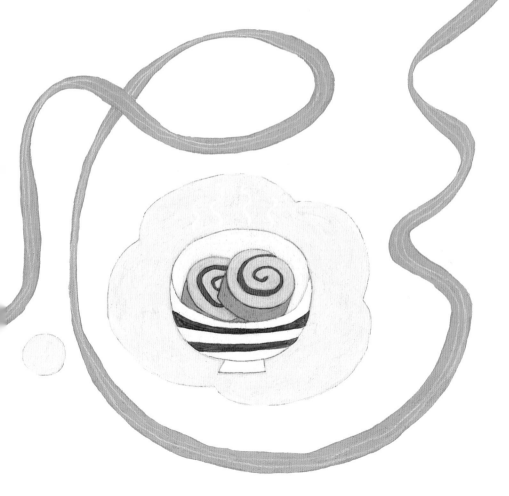

Suddenly Nipper heard
noises above his head. They
sounded like the scampering
feet of a whole pack of...rats!

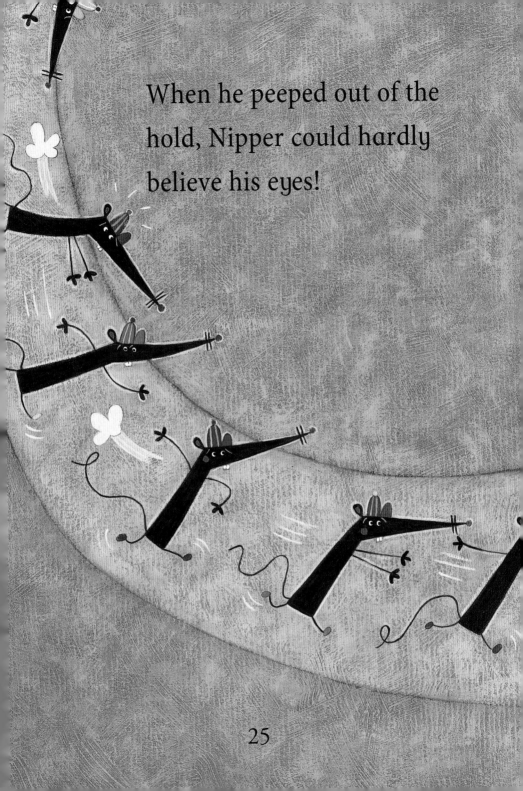

When he peeped out of the
hold, Nipper could hardly
believe his eyes!

There was only one thing to do. Nipper had to go home. When the coast was clear, he crept up the stairs and onto the deck.

He was just in time.

The ship was about to sail.

As the hooter went off,

Nipper slid, paw over paw,

down the rope and back

onto the dockside.

Nipper stood and watched as the ship slowly sailed away. He waved goodbye to his old enemies who were madly trying to escape.

"Get Nipper!" the rats squealed.
But it was too late for that.

Then Nipper turned and headed for home. Perhaps by now his mother would have forgotten that she'd grounded him.

If he hurried he might not miss supper. It was Friday and Mrs McFee always made toad-in-the-hole – *with real toads.* *Mmm*, Nipper's favourite!

ROSE IMPEY MELANIE WILLIAMSON

All priced at £8.99

Orchard Books are available from all good bookshops,
or can be ordered from our website: www.orchardbooks.co.uk,
or telephone 01235 827702, or fax 01235 827703.

Prices and availability are subject to change.